THE WARLOCK'S STAFF

KorakA
THE WINGED
ASSASSIN

With special thanks to Cherith Baldry

To Henry

www.beastquest.co.uk

ORCHARD BOOKS
338 Euston Road, London NW1 3BH
Orchard Books Australia
Level 17/207 Kent St, Sydney, NSW 2000

A Paperback Original
First published in Great Britain in 2011

A CIP catalogue record for this book is available from
the British Library.

ISBN 978 1 40831 318 3

Printed and bound in China by Imago

The paper and board used in this paperback are natural recyclable
products made from wood grown in sustainable forests. The
manufacturing processes conform to the environmental regulations of
the country of origin.

Orchard Books is a division of Hachette Children's Books,
an Hachette UK company

www.hachette.co.uk

KORAKA
THE WINGED
ASSASSIN

BY ADAM BLADE

ORCHARD

THE ETERNAL FLAME

THE SEA OF SERAPH

THE SNOWY NORTH

FISHING VILLAGE

THE RAGING RIVER

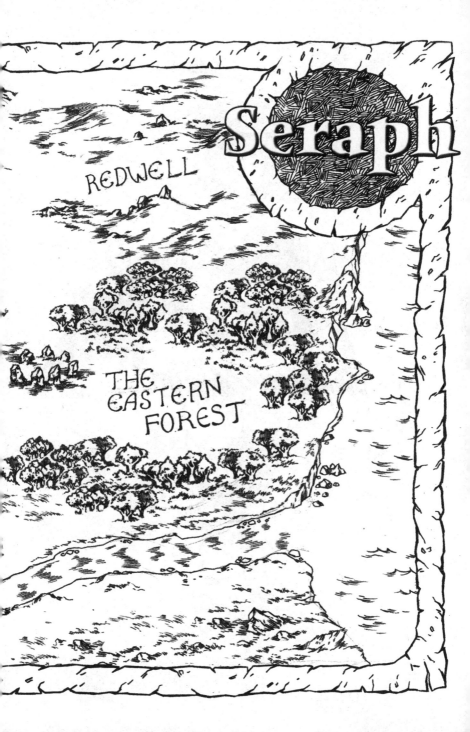

*T*om and Elenna are such fools! They thought their Quests were over and that my master was defeated. They were wrong! For now Malvel has the Warlock's Staff, hewn from the Tree of Being, and all kingdoms will soon be at his mercy.

We travel the land of Seraph, to find the Eternal Flame. And when we burn the Staff in the flame, our evil magic will be unstoppable. Tom and Elenna can chase us if they wish, but they'll find more than just Beasts lying in wait. They're alone this time, with no wizard to help them.

I hope Tom and Elenna are ready to meet me again. I've been waiting a long time for my revenge.

Yours, with glee, Petra the Witch

PROLOGUE

Cora the shepherdess glanced up at the morning sun. "I'm so late," she muttered, thumping the end of her shepherd's crook against the ground to spur her flock on faster. "The market will be over before I get there."

She hurried along the grassy path through the hills. Her flock of sheep trotted ahead of her, filling the air with their gentle bleating. Overhead the sky was a clear blue, with only a few wisps of cloud.

Cora gazed ahead for her first sight of Redwell, the little market town in the west of Seraph where she would sell her sheep. The ground was soft beneath her aching feet, which slipped on the grass and mud as she broke into a run.

"I have to keep going," she muttered. "I must get—"

Cora felt the ground give way under her feet. She landed on hard, uneven earth, a shower of grass and thin branches tumbled with her. For a moment she was stunned, and couldn't see for the dirt in her eyes. Her right ankle was in agony from her awkward fall. When she wiped her eyes clear, she looked around and saw that she had dropped into a pit with steep sides.

Shaking off the scattered grass, Cora struggled to stand. She clawed her way up one of the earth walls, pain stabbing through her ankle.

"Help!" she called. "Someone help me out of here!"

But the only reply was Cora's own voice bouncing back at her, echoing off the hillsides. Nobody lived in these deserted hills. The nearest help was a long way off, in Redwell.

From up above, Cora could hear the frightened bleating of her sheep, and the drumming of their hooves as they scattered.

Oh, no! she thought. *If I lose the flock, I won't get paid.*

Cora grabbed at stones stuck in the wall in an effort to climb out. But it was too steep and the stones came away in her hands. When she tried to dig out a foothold, the earth walls of the pit simply crumbled.

Who would do something like this? Cora asked herself. *Didn't they realise someone would fall in?*

The pit went dark. Cora blinked and looked up. A girl stood at the edge, gazing down. Her short, plump body blocked out the sunlight, casting her face in shadow.

"Oh, thank goodness!" Cora exclaimed, relief surging through her. "I thought no one would find me. I'm so lucky you happened to be passing."

As Cora's eyes adjusted to the shadow, she saw the girl's face more clearly. It was wide and round, framed by long, greasy hair that hung down as she leaned over the edge into the pit. She was smiling.

"Hello," she said. "I'm Petra. Let me help you."

Petra leaned over further and reached down her chubby arm.

Cora stood on tiptoe and managed to grasp it. "Thank you," she said. "What type of fool would dig a pit in the middle of this field?"

Cora waited for Petra to pull her up, but she did not. The girl just held Cora's hand tight, her helpful smile fading to a look of cruel malice.

"Me," the girl cackled, lashing out with her free arm. Cora saw a flash of steel just as agony exploded through her shoulder.

Cora fell back into the pit, collapsing on her bad ankle. She looked up, gasping in pain, and saw that Petra clutched a knife with a purple blade.

"Why did you do that?" Cora cried. "I haven't done you any harm!"

Petra just giggled. Cora stared in disbelief as the shape of the girl seemed to waver and then broke apart like water hitting rock. All that remained was the echo of her laughter, and a few wisps of purple smoke.

"Magic!" Cora breathed, unable to believe what she had just seen. She started to stand up again, when the pain in her shoulder became too immense. She looked at her wound. Her skin stretched and swelled. With a lurch of fear, Cora saw feathers burst from the gash.

A fierce pressure was building at the bottom of her back. It felt as if her skin was stretching and stretching until at last it would explode.

She let out a whimper of pain and terror.

Breathless with shock, Cora caught sight of her shadow on the wall of the pit. Her back was swelling, curving. Something was growing out of it.

"I'm growing wings!" she gasped in disbelief.

The rest of Cora's body began to swell. Her leather trousers and shirt tore as she outgrew them, and her boots split with a harsh tearing sound as claws slid out from her feet. A feathered tail erupted from her lower back.

And it wasn't just her body. Even her shepherd's crook changed, growing into a spear with a glittering point.

As the agony grew, Cora's mind blanked out. She couldn't remember who she was any more. The pain faded, and her whole body was filled with a desperate hunger.

The pit had been barely big enough for her to begin with; now she was straining against the sides, making it wider. She raised her wings, beating down strongly.

Cora was gone.

I am Koraka!

CHAPTER ONE

HUNGER PANGS

Tom urged Storm into a canter as they
headed across the plain, with Silver
loping alongside. He stretched his
aching muscles, loosening up after his
battle against Minos the Demon Bull.

"I can't believe how hard it was to
defeat Minos!" he said.

"I know." Elenna, mounted on
Storm behind Tom, gripped his waist
a little tighter. "And our Quest is

going to get harder still."

A shudder of fear shook Tom as he thought of what would happen if they failed. The evil wizard Malvel had stolen the Warlock's Staff from Avantia, and he intended to burn it in the Eternal Flame, here in the land of Seraph.

"If Malvel succeeds," Elenna said, "then he'll have ultimate power over all the known worlds. And we'll never see Aduro again."

Tom felt the icy touch of dread as he remembered the awful moment back in Avantia when the Good Wizard Aduro vanished and his robes crumpled, empty, to the ground.

Aduro's life is linked to the Staff, he thought. *We must get it back to Avantia before it's too late.*

"We'll have to make sure Malvel

doesn't succeed," Tom said, hands clenching the reins. "Let's have another look at the map, and see where we have to go next."

Elenna rummaged in Storm's saddlebag. Tom drew Storm to a halt so that he could study the map with Elenna. A silvery line had appeared, leading across the plain and into a hilly region a little way to the north-east. Above the hills was the tiny picture of a winged creature. Beneath it, the word *Koraka* appeared.

"It looks a bit like an eagle," Tom said.

"But it's got arms as well as wings," said Elenna. "And look at the spear it's carrying. It could rip us apart!"

"That's our next Beast," Tom said. "Let's go!"

He dug his heels into Storm's sides, urging him across the plain at a gallop. Silver let out an excited yelp and forged ahead.

Tom could make out the outline of the hills on the horizon. At their foot, he saw the roof of a farmhouse. Trees were planted in rows around it, and corn grew in lush fields. Anger surged through Tom. Seraph was a beautiful realm, and Malvel was trying to destroy it in his quest for power.

Well, I won't let him, Tom thought.

As Storm cantered on, Tom felt Elenna's head slump onto his shoulder.

"Elenna?" Tom stiffened in alarm. "What's the matter?"

Elenna raised her head a little, then let it flop back onto Tom's shoulder. "So…hungry…" she moaned.

"I know," Tom replied. His own stomach was hollow. He couldn't remember the last time they had eaten. *How long can we keep going?* He worried that they might not be strong enough to defeat Malvel's Beasts when the time came.

"There must be some way of getting food," he said, shielding his eyes with one hand as he squinted into the distance. He saw trees planted in rows. "It looks as if there are orchards over there, near that farm."

"Then let's see if we can get some fruit," Elenna suggested, sitting up again. She sounded more hopeful.

Tom tugged on Storm's reins to turn the stallion towards the orchard. His mouth watered, thinking of juicy red apples or succulent pears nestling among the leaves. But as they drew nearer, his hope turned to despair. All the apples had been shaken free from the trees and lay rotting on the ground.

Tom stared down at the black, bruised and mushy fruit. "Ugh! Why has it been left to rot like this?

Elenna pointed weakly at broken branches on the ground. "Something's shaken the fruit loose," she said. "And look at those markings on the trunk!"

Sure enough, there were deep pale gouges in the bark.

Almost like claw-marks, Tom thought.

"It's hopeless," Elenna said miserably. "We're going to starve to death here."

Silver let out a mournful howl, as if he was sharing her disappointment.

"I don't want to turn aside from our Quest," Tom said. "Who knows what damage the Beast will do? But we can't defeat Malvel if we're weak from hunger."

"And if we fail, Aduro will be lost for ever," Elenna murmured.

She's right, Tom thought. *I wish I knew what to do. Do I search for the Beast right away, or look for some food first? If I make the wrong decision, our Quest is finished...*

CHAPTER TWO

LAMBS TO THE SLAUGHTER

"We can't go on without looking for some food," Tom said. He was worried that Elenna might faint again, and next time she wouldn't recover so quickly. He was also feeling very weak. "We need to find a town."

Urging Storm on, Tom headed for the hills. Soon the land began to rise, the rich grass of the plains giving way to tough moorland turf.

"This is near the place where the map said we would find the Beast," Elenna pointed out.

Tom gazed up at the sky, but there was no sign of the winged creature with the spear. "We can't worry about that just now," he said. "We need to build up our strength first."

Tom cast glances from side to side as they rode on. He kept looking up, half-expecting the Beast to appear, but the sky remained clear – there wasn't even a single bird.

Maybe they're too scared of the Beast to stay around here, Tom thought.

Tom guided Storm along a grassy path that led through the hills, spurring the stallion to a gallop. The land of Seraph slid beneath Storm's hooves in a blur of green.

Tom saw a flicker of black on the ground ahead. Instinctively he wrenched on Storm's reins. The stallion veered sharply to one side.

"Hey!" Elenna cried out, grabbing hard at Tom's shoulders.

Glancing back, Tom saw that his friend had almost fallen out of the saddle. When she was steady again, he brought Storm to a stop, leaning forward to pat his glossy black neck.

"Sorry, boy," he said. "Take it easy. Let's see what that is."

Looking down, Tom saw that they were standing on the edge of a pit. Silver sniffed at the edge, peering down.

"Stay here, boy," Elenna said sharply. "Don't jump in there."

The sides of the pit were bare earth,

with deep marks scored down them.
Dead grass and a few thin branches
were scattered over the bottom.

"It must be a trap," Elenna said.
"The grass and the branches would
have been laid over the top to hide
the pit."

Tom frowned. "Who would do
that? And what was it meant to
trap?"

"Robbers? Dangerous animals?"
Elenna glanced round nervously.

"I don't know," Tom replied. "The
grass down there isn't dead yet, so
the pit was only dug a short time
ago. We'll need to be careful, in case
there are any more." He shivered at
the thought of Storm falling into a pit
and breaking one of his legs.

"This must be one of the more
dangerous parts of Seraph," Elenna
said.

"But at least we're warned now,"
Tom said, squaring his shoulders.

He set Storm moving, more slowly
now, and scanned the ground ahead
for traces of any more traps. But
the grassy path was smooth and
unbroken.

"Look over there," Elenna said,
pointing to the side of the road

a little way ahead. "Is that snow?"

Tom looked where she was pointing and saw a white patch standing out against the green grass. It looked like a small pocket of snow.

"That's odd," he murmured. "The weather's quite mild, and there's no sign of snow anywhere else."

Tom kept a careful eye on the ground ahead. Before they had gone very far, they came upon the patch of snow. Except, it wasn't snow – it was sheep's wool.

"Oh, no..." Elenna whispered, horror in her voice. "Something has been killing the sheep."

"Maybe the Beast." Tom's spine prickled, as if he could feel Malvel's evil creature watching him. But when he looked up at the sky there was still no trace of it.

A whine from Silver made Tom look down at the ground again. The grey wolf was standing a little further along the path, his nose down to sniff something in the grass.

"What has he found?" Elenna asked.

Drawing closer, Tom spotted sticky red splotches leading up the hillside, and caught the smell of blood on the air.

"Something – or someone – has been wounded," he said.

Elenna tugged at Tom's shoulder: "They might need help."

Tom nodded, and turned Storm aside to follow the smears of blood up the slope. The trail led to a shallow dip in the ground. At the bottom, a sheep lay on its side, motionless. At first Tom thought it was dead, but as he began to guide Storm carefully down towards it, the sheep struggled weakly to get up, then sank back again with a feeble bleat.

"I think you were right," Tom told Elenna. "Maybe this is a more savage part of Seraph."

"I don't understand," Elenna replied, peering around Tom to gaze down sadly at the dying sheep. "Seraph is such a beautiful realm."

"It was until Malvel disturbed it," said Tom grimly.

He jumped down from Storm and stooped beside the animal. Now that he was close to it, he could see deep cuts on its body, as if fierce claws had scored through its woolly fleece.

"A Beast did this," he said.

Tom looked up at the sky again.

I can feel Koraka's close, he thought. *But why can't I see it?*

Warning Silver to stay back, Elenna dismounted and crouched by the sheep's head, stroking it gently. "Look at her belly," she said. "I think she's carrying a lamb."

Tom gazed down at the helpless sheep, clenching his fists with anger at the thought of the innocent creature being hurt. "We can't let her die!" he burst out.

Returning to Storm, he unhooked his shield from the saddle and took out the talon he had received from Epos the Flame Bird, which had the ability to heal wounds.

"I hope this works," he said as he knelt beside the sheep again, touching the talon against the gashes. Relief flooded over him as he saw them begin to close.

"I've seen that happen so often," he murmured, "and it still seems wonderful!"

Elenna nodded, running her hand over the sheep's side as wool sprouted from where the claw marks had been. "Look – even her fleece has grown back!"

The sheep scrambled to her feet and trotted away, looking as happy and healthy as if she had never been injured.

"My tokens seem to be even more powerful in Seraph than they were in Avantia," Tom commented as he watched her.

Even though Elenna still looked pale and strained from hunger, her face broke into a wide grin. It faded quickly as the sound of slow clapping rattled through the air. Springing to his feet, Tom spun round to see an image of Malvel floating above his head. The wizard's shape covered half the sky, swirling as if it was formed out of smoke. The evil wizard's malevolent eyes gleamed from beneath his hood and in one hand

he flourished the Warlock's Staff.

"What a hero you are, Tom!" Malvel's voice was harsh and sarcastic. "You've saved one measly sheep!"

"It's better than destroying things," Tom snapped back. "The only thing I'll ever destroy is you."

"Oh, really?" Malvel sneered. "Watch this, little hero. Your Quest is over!"

Tom's eyes stretched wide with horror and he felt his chest tighten as a new image began to build around the shape of Malvel: a circle of golden flames like the petals of a flower.

"The Eternal Flame!" Elenna gasped.

"How clever you are," Malvel said, his words falling into a cackle of mocking laughter.

Too shocked to speak, Tom watched until the last trace of Malvel's shape, and the flames that surrounded him, had vanished, leaving behind only the echo of his laughter.

"Malvel has reached the Eternal Flame!" Elenna's voice was shaking. "Does that mean that all is lost?"

CHAPTER THREE

THE EMPTY HOUSE

"I don't believe it," Tom said. "If Malvel had really reached the Eternal Flame, he would be all powerful. He wouldn't need to put a Beast in our path. Don't be fooled, Elenna. He's just trying to make us give up."

As he spoke, his friend's face cleared, and she began to smile. "But we won't!" she exclaimed.

"Never," Tom agreed, slipping

Epos's talon back into his shield. Then he mounted Storm again and pulled Elenna up behind him. "Now to look for some food," he said.

The grassy path they'd been following through the hills shortly joined a dirt road. Rounding the foot of a crag, Tom could make out the walls of a small town in the valley ahead. Behind the wall he could see a jumble of roof-tops with smoke rising from fires.

"More sheep have been along this way," said Elenna, pointing to tufts of wool caught on the thorny bushes that lined the road.

Tom nodded. He had also spotted countless hoofprints in the dried mud of the road. "Flocks of sheep have been driven along here," he said. "The injured sheep we saw must have been part of a flock destroyed by the Beast. That means the town ahead is probably a market town."

"We might be able to find food there," Elenna added.

Tom urged Storm into a faster trot. He was feeling optimistic too. So far the people of Seraph they had met had been friendly and ready to help. Surely, if they knocked on a door and asked politely, someone would spare them something.

The first house they came to stood a little way away from the edge of town. Tom's stomach growled as he sniffed the tasty smells drifting through the window. He imagined a pot of rich soup or a juicy haunch of meat turning on a spit.

"This seems like a good place," he said as he dismounted Storm and hurried up to the door. He knocked.

There was no reply.

"Oh no," Elenna said as she joined him. "There must be someone there! My stomach's never felt so empty."

Tom knocked again but still no one came to answer. He exchanged a glance with Elenna, then lifted the latch and cautiously pushed the door open. "Is anyone at home?" he called.

The door led into a large kitchen with a stone-flagged floor. Bundles of herbs and vegetables hung from the ceiling. At the opposite side of the room an iron cooking pot hung over a small fire, with delicious-smelling steam wafting from it.

"Do you think we could take some food?" Elenna suggested. "We could leave something behind as payment."

Tom hesitated. He didn't like the

idea of helping themselves when the
owner of the house was away. *But
we're desperate*, he reminded himself.

"If we starve, there'll be no one to
stop Malvel," he said, making up his
mind. "We'll leave the golden harp
that we used to defeat Ursus. We
don't need it anymore."

"Right," said Elenna, "and it's worth
more than a couple of bowls of food."

Tom unfastened his sword belt and propped his sword against the doorpost. Then he stepped forward into the kitchen, with Elenna close behind him. Bowls were set out on a table in the middle of the floor. Elenna held two of them while Tom grabbed a ladle that hung by the fire.

Elenna peered into the pot. "Parsnip soup. My favourite!"

Tom ladled soup into each bowl. "I'll fetch the harp before we eat," he said. "That way we can—"

Tom fell silent at the crunch of footsteps on the path outside. The room grew dark as a shadow fell over Tom. He glanced towards the doorway and saw a large, angry-looking man. His hair and bushy beard were black, and he wore a shabby leather jerkin over a thick woollen shirt and trousers.

"What's going on here?" he demanded. Tom opened his mouth to reply but the man didn't let him speak. "I nip off to call my son for dinner, and I come back to find thieves in my home!"

"It's not what you think. We just—" Tom began.

Ignoring Silver's growls, the man picked up Tom's sword from where he had left it leaning against the doorpost, drew it from its scabbard, and brandished it clumsily.

"Get out of my house!" he snarled.

He took a pace back, making room for Tom and Elenna to leave, but keeping the sword firmly trained on them. Tom stepped out with his eyes fixed on the gleaming blade. Elenna set down the bowls on the table and followed.

As they emerged into the open air,
Tom spotted a small boy running
down the road that led to the town.

"Fredo!" the man bellowed. "Go
and get the townsfolk! We've got
thieves in here!"

"No, wait!" Tom protested, but
the boy spun round right away
and pelted back towards the town.
"We were going to pay."

"I've heard that story before," the man yelled. "You'll soon find out what we do with thieves around here." He swung the sword tip to and fro, pointing from Tom to Elenna and back again until the little boy came running back. A dozen strong men came with him, all armed with clubs and stout sticks.

"These two were in my house, stealing food," the man said, as the townsfolk crowded around Tom and Elenna. Two of the men grabbed Tom, while two of the others seized Elenna. Tom struggled, but he couldn't break free. When he looked at Elenna he saw that she was too weak from hunger to put up a fight.

"Right," one of the men said with a threatening look at Tom. "It's the stocks for you two!"

CHAPTER FOUR

IN THE STOCKS!

The men dragged Tom and Elenna towards the road. Storm let out a whinny as another of the men grabbed his bridle, rearing up and striking the air with his forehooves, and almost dragging the man off his feet. Then as Tom and Elenna were hauled away, Storm grew quieter, and let the man lead him along behind.

Yet another man turned to Silver, a hand outstretched to grab him by the ruff, only to back away when the wolf bared his teeth in a fierce snarl.

"Well done, boy!" Elenna called. "Don't let them touch you!"

Silver backed away, then darted between the safety of two buildings.

At least one of us is still free, Tom thought.

The townsfolk hustled Tom and Elenna into the town and along a wide street until they came to a square. Market stalls were set out around the sides, roofed by striped canvas awnings and shaded by trees. In the middle were two sets of stocks.

"You've got this all wrong," Tom protested as their captors dragged him and Elenna across the square. "If you'd only listen, I can explain."

One of the men gripping his arm let out a loud guffaw. "I'll wager you can, lad," he said. "But Cris caught you thieving, and that's good enough for me."

The black-bearded man, Cris, was already heaving off the top bar of the stocks. Tom's captors shoved his neck and wrists into the holes, and the top bar came down with a loud thump.

Glancing to one side, he saw Cris

fastening the bars together with thick loops of rope. Beside him, more of the men were pushing Elenna into the other set of stocks. She hung there with her head drooping, as though asleep standing up.

Tom felt a chill of terror in his chest. *Malvel could reach the Eternal Flame while we're stuck here!*

The man who had led Storm into the square was lashing him to the branch of a nearby tree by his reins. "This is a fine horse," he remarked.

"Yes, and he'll be finer still when we've butchered him and shared out the meat," another of the townspeople replied. "That'll help to make up for the sheep we lost when Cora never turned up."

"Don't you dare!" Tom yelled, straining uselessly against the stocks.

"I'd not be surprised if this pair know something about how Cora disappeared," Cris said to one of his friends. He turned to Tom with a threatening look. "What do you know about Cora the shepherdess, boy?"

"I've never heard of her!" Tom replied, but he could see that no one believed him.

Tom looked around for Silver, and at first he couldn't see him. Then he spotted him crouching underneath one of the market stalls. He snapped at anyone who came near him; Tom could see that they were all too frightened of him to drag him out.

"Huh!" one of the men muttered as he walked away. "Leave him there. I don't like wolf meat anyway!"

More townsfolk were pouring into

the square, crowding round the stocks to point and jeer at Tom and Elenna. Tom tried to ignore them, still straining to see what was happening to Storm.

Something slammed into Tom's face. Stunned, he glanced down to see a rotten apple sliding from his chin down the front of his tunic. He looked up again to see a line

of townsfolk, more rotting fruit and vegetables in their hands. They were taking aim.

"No!" Tom yelled.

The townsfolk ignored his protest. They hurled their stinking missiles at Tom and Elenna's faces.

A squashy melon burst open on Tom's face, drenching him in putrid pulp. He shook his head to clear the

juice out of his eyes. When his vision cleared, he spotted a familiar figure crouching behind a barrel.

"Petra!" he choked.

The young witch looked up at him and grinned. She was hidden from the rest of the villagers behind a barrel. With a wave of her hand she conjured up a turnip and flung it at Tom. It bounced off the top of his head. An onion spun through the air and hit Elenna. Petra's grin grew wider as she spread her hands and attacked them both with a vicious barrage of rotting fruit and vegetables.

"Enjoy your meal!" she taunted them with a giggle.

"Coward!" Tom spluttered, spitting out bits of mouldy cabbage. "Why don't you let us out of the stocks,

so we can have a fair fight?"

Petra let out a sneering laugh.
"Why would I do that? Stop trying
to speak to my sense of honour, Tom.
I haven't got one, and that's just the
way I like it." She hurled a worm-
eaten potato that slammed into the
bar of the stocks and landed on
Tom's head.

"I'll get you for this," Tom hissed
through clenched teeth. "As long as

there's blood in my veins I'll seek you out and make you pay."

A wicked smile broke out on Petra's face. "There won't be blood in your veins for much longer," she said. "Look up – oh, I forgot. You can't."

But Tom didn't need to look up to know that danger was close. A thick shadow slid across the square, casting it in darkness.

Koraka is here.

All around the square the townsfolk were staring up in horror, letting out terrified cries as they tried to flee.

"Help! Save me!"

"What is it?"

"Get out of my way!"

They pushed and shoved to get out of the square or into the buildings that surrounded it. Some of them dived for refuge under the market stalls.

Tom heaved against the stocks with all his strength, but he couldn't break the thick rope.

We're helpless, he thought, grinding his teeth in frustration. *And there's a Beast about to tear the town apart!*

CHAPTER FIVE

TERROR FROM THE SKY

Tom strained to look upwards. All he could see was a pair of cruel talons, like an eagle's, flashing past him as the Beast swooped over the square. The claws sank into the shoulders of a man who struggled to escape the fierce grip. A smell of decaying flesh wafted over Tom.

Losing sight of the Beast again,

Tom made another effort to break free of the stocks, but it was useless.

I need to think of something. But short of growing an extra arm to untie the rope, what can I do?

Then Tom spotted Silver leaping out from beneath the market stall. None of the terrified crowd noticed him now. Tom felt a rush of relief and triumph – they could always count on their wolf friend.

"Elenna!" he called urgently. "Whistle for Silver!"

Elenna raised her head and she smiled as she spotted the grey wolf. She pursed her lips into a shrill whistle and then called, "Here, boy!"

Silver bounded across the square, dodging between the legs of the crowd, until he reached the stocks where Elenna was trapped. Standing on his hind legs, he bit at the rope.

"I knew you'd help us," said Elenna, her voice strained and weary.

Within seconds, Silver had gnawed through the ropes that held Elenna's stocks. Elenna was able to heave up the heavy bar and free herself. At once she hurried over to Tom's stocks, untied his ropes and helped him lift his bar up.

"Thanks, Elenna," Tom gasped, massaging his wrists and neck. "Thanks, Silver."

The wolf bounded across to where Storm was still tied to the tree, and tugged at his reins until the stallion was free. Then both their animal friends made their way back to Tom and Elenna. Tom's heart sank as he realised that Cris still had his sword. His shield wasn't hanging in its place on Storm's saddle, and Elenna's bow and arrows had disappeared too.

How am I supposed to fight a Beast without my weapons? he thought.

"There's no time to lose," he said. "We have to help these people."

Looking up, he got a good look at the Beast for the first time. She had the body of a human woman, lean and muscular, but far too big for the

tattered shirt and leather trousers
that strained to stay on her limbs.

"She's so tall!" Elenna exclaimed.

Parts of the Beast's body were
covered by feathers. An eagle's tail
sprouted from her lower back, and
powerful wings stretched up from
her shoulderblades. In one hand,
she carried a vicious-looking spear,
which she raked across the canopy
of a market stall as she swooped low.
The wooden frame tumbled down
and the canvas awnings fell to the
ground in ragged ribbons.

"Her head looks almost human..."
Tom murmured. The Beast's mouth
was a gaping hole, ringed with
needle-sharp teeth. But her eyes
were green, and strangely beautiful
in the horror of her body.

"I wonder if she was human once,

before Malvel and Petra used their
magic to transform her," Elenna said.

Tom nodded. "If she was, we'll
bring her back."

The square swarmed with people
as they tried to flee. Some huddled
behind the stocks or hammered on

the doors of the buildings around the square, yelling to be let in. A man stumbled past Tom with blood pouring from scratches on his back and shoulders.

Tom spotted Cris, the man whose house he and Elenna had entered. He wasn't running away - he was pushing his way through the crowd, searching behind the trees and stooping to look underneath the market stalls.

"Fredo! Fredo!" he called.

Tom grabbed him. "Where are our weapons?" he demanded.

Cris gazed at them and Tom could see fear had snatched away his senses.

"Our weapons!" Tom repeated, giving the man a shake. "We can stop this creature."

Cris blinked as if he was waking up.

"My son is missing," he explained. "I'll give you your weapons back if you help me look for him."

"Of course we will," said Elenna.

Tom gazed around. By now the square was starting to clear, and it didn't take him long to spot Fredo hiding behind a tree. But just as Tom was about to call out to Cris, a shadow fell over the boy. Before Tom could react, he heard the fierce rush of air from the Beast's wings as she swooped down on the cowering Fredo. The tree groaned as the Beast tore it up with one clawed foot, while with the other she grabbed Fredo. The boy let out a shrill scream as the Beast carried him upwards.

"No!" Cris shouted, shaking his fists helplessly. "She took my son!"

Frozen with horror, Tom and

Elenna stood staring upwards as the
Beast mounted high into the sky.
Fredo screamed and writhed, but
soon his voice faded and the
struggling figure was just a tiny
dot in the sky.

CHAPTER SIX

THE BEAST'S NEST

Tom grasped Cris's arm. "Give us our weapons back," he said, "and I promise we'll save your son."

Cris looked at him with a haunted expression. "How can you do that?" he asked, shaking his head helplessly. "How can a boy fight that...thing?"

"I've met creatures like her before," Tom told him.

A spark of hope appeared in Cris's

eyes. "Can you really promise that you won't fail?"

"I've never failed," Tom assured him. "And I don't intend to start now."

"Just hurry!" Elenna begged.

"Wait here," said Cris.

He ran across the square and ducked into a small building. When he reappeared he was carrying Tom's sword and shield, and Elenna's bow and her quiver of arrows.

"Here," he said, holding them out. "And if you can get Fredo back, you can name your own reward."

"I don't do this for the reward," Tom told him as he buckled on his sword belt and slipped his shield onto his arm.

Elenna slung her bow and quiver over her shoulder. Then they both mounted Storm and galloped out of the square. Silver scampering behind through the dust thrown up from the stallion's hooves.

Tom could still make out the distant shape of the Beast outlined against the sky. She was heading towards the hills. As Tom and Elenna followed, the path grew steeper until they were travelling among sheer crags of grey rock. Storm's hooves clinked on loose stones, and Tom slowed him to a walk.

"These mountains look as dangerous as any I've seen," he said to Elenna.

"I know," Elenna agreed. "We'll need to be careful. If we—"

Tom looked round sharply when loud, shrill laughter sounded on the air.

Petra stepped onto the path from behind the rock. Hands on hips, she started to walk towards Tom with a sneer on her face.

Rage surged through him as he remembered how Petra had taunted him and hurled fruit and vegetables while he was captive in the stocks. Leaning down from the saddle, he drew his sword. "Stay away from us!"

Petra moved right alongside them and waved her hand over the blade. It passed right through.

"She's just a vision!" said Elenna.

"You two aren't the brightest minds in Avantia, are you?" said Petra, tossing back her greasy hair. "Would I put myself in danger? Of course I wouldn't. I just wanted to have a look at what you're doing. You don't really think you have a chance against Koraka, do you?"

Tom bit back a yell of fury and pointed his sword at Petra. "I'll overcome this Beast," he vowed. "And one day I'll wipe the smile off your face, too."

"Sure you will," Petra sneered, as her form grew thinner, until Tom could see the rocks behind her. Her eerie giggle still echoed among the rocks after she had vanished like mist.

Tom urged Storm forward again, but the path they were following grew narrower still and finally dwindled to a rocky track that zig-zagged up the mountainside.

"We'll have to climb from here," Elenna said.

Tom nodded. "The hill is too treacherous for Storm," he said, sliding out of the saddle. "And I think you should stay here with him and Silver. I know you're not afraid to face Koraka," he went on, seeing that Elenna was about to protest. "But there's no sense in both of us risking our lives. If I fail, or fall, you will have to carry on the Quest."

Elenna hesitated for a moment. Tom could see she was reluctant to let him face danger alone. "All right," she replied at last. "Good luck!"

Slinging his shield onto his back, Tom set off up the steep hill. Before long, even the narrow track disappeared and he had to climb, searching for hand and footholds in the sheer rock.

It's a good thing I've travelled in mountains before, he thought.

Tom climbed higher and higher, until the air grew thin and his chest began to ache. He dared to look down. He could not see Elenna anymore. He could barely see his own feet for the misty wisps of white that curled around them.

I'm higher than the clouds, he realised.

From somewhere in the distance, Tom's ears picked up an eerie shriek and the sound of sobbing. He forced himself to keep going, to keep looking for the next crack in the rock. His limbs were weak from hunger and exertion, quivering so much that Tom worried he might fall.

It would make sense to stop, he thought. *But I mustn't. I've promised to rescue Fredo.*

At last Tom dragged himself onto level ground. His chest heaved as he sucked in deep breaths. Through the wisps of cloud he could see in front of him a curious deep trough in the hill, with claw-marks scored along the sides.

"That's not natural," he muttered out loud. "It must be the work of the Beast."

Then the cloud lifted a little so that Tom could see into the depths of the trough. A shiver ran through him when he saw that the dip in the land

was lined with what looked like
white sticks. Tom felt sick with
disgust when he realised what it was.

A nest of bones!

Amid tattered scraps of bloodied
fleece, trying to wriggle free, was
Fredo.

CHAPTER SEVEN
A DARING RESCUE

Fredo was surrounded by the bones and skulls of sheep, picked free of meat. He looked like a fly trapped in a spider's web.

Taking a deep breath, Tom steadied himself. He slid his shield onto his arm and drew his sword as he glanced all around. But there was no sign of Koraka through the thick clouds that rolled about him. But that didn't mean she was hidden just behind them, ready to pounce.

I've got to be careful, he thought.

Crouching low, Tom crept along the hill-top, round the rim of the trough, until he drew closer to the place where Fredo was lying. The boy hadn't seen him yet. The sparse moorland grass was wet and the stones slick with dampness from the clouds. It would be very easy for Tom to slip and fall right off the hill – and he wouldn't survive a drop like that.

At last he reached a spot on the rim just above the place where Fredo lay trapped. He was too far away to reach down to him.

The little boy's face was streaked with tears. He was whimpering in terror, and his clothes were torn, but didn't seem to be badly hurt.

"Fredo!" Tom kept his voice low, for fear of alerting Koraka, and waved his sword to get the boy's attention.

Fredo spotted him and opened his mouth to cry out. Tom put a finger to his lips. To his relief Fredo nodded and clamped his mouth tight shut to control his frightened sobs.

Tom listened for the sound of wings, but everything was silent.

Maybe Koraka went back to the town, he thought.

Cautiously Tom let himself down into the trough and edged towards Fredo through the nest of bones. He winced as his feet crunched on the debris, but he couldn't be any quieter.

Tom drew closer to Fredo, until he was only a few paces away. Still the Beast was nowhere to be seen.

Tom raised his sword to start

cutting away the bones that trapped
Fredo. His sword went through them
easily – the boy would soon be free.
As Tom reached out a hand to him,
Fredo's eyes widened.

Whoosh!

Koraka's talons stabbed down
through the cloud in a blur. The
Beast landed on the edge of the
trough, punching deep holes into the
mountaintop. The whole nest rattled
under Tom's feet as though it had
been shaken by a mighty earthquake.

Fredo let out a terrified cry. Tom
recoiled and backward-rolled onto
his feet, his sword and shield ready.

But Koraka had vanished. Tom
stared round, knowing that she was
hovering somewhere, out of his
reach and hidden by the thick cloud.

The Beast dipped through the cloud

cover again, landing just in front of
Tom. Tom leapt backwards, nearly
losing his balance. He swung at Koraka,
but his sword found only air when the
Beast hovered higher. Her cruel claws
raked down, either side of Tom's head,
and he scrambled out of the way.

With a throat-ripping roar, Tom
hacked his sword at Koraka's thick,
scaly leg. But the blade bounced off,

shaking in Tom's hands. The Beast looped back in the air, as if Tom had tried to attack her with a feather.

Avoiding another strike of the talons, Tom dove aside, rolling down into the depths of the bone nest. The sickening stench filled his nose, making him gag and his chest heave. Crawling to Fredo, he chopped and pulled at the remaining bones until Fredo could scramble up.

"What are we going to do?" the little boy asked, his eyes wide with terror and his voice shaking. "She'll never let us go!"

"We'll find a way," Tom said.

At least Koraka seemed to have drawn off. But Tom wasn't sure how he was going to get Fredo down from the mountain. The climb up, on his own, had been tricky enough. It was a long way down, and the terrain was treacherous.

One slip, and we're going to fall, Tom thought. To balance better, he shifted the position of his shield on his shoulder. Tom felt a grin come over his face. *My shield*, he thought, triumphantly. *I have Arcta's eagle feather, to protect me from great falls. There is hope!*

"Hold on tight!" Tom told Fredo, sheathing his sword.

As the little boy gripped him tightly round the waist, Tom raised his shield into the air and turned to face the clouds, and the impossible drop to the land below.

He felt Fredo's fingers almost tear through his tunic. "What are you going to—"

Tom did not let Fredo finish his

question. He ran up the side of the trough, dragging Fredo with him, and leaped off the mountainside.

Fredo wailed in fear.

"It's all right!" Tom called over the rush of air, and the flap of their clothes on the wind.

The power of Arcta's feather in Tom's shield caused them to drift down slowly. Recovering from his panic, Fredo gazed around curiously.

"We're flying!" he cried.

"Not quite," Tom replied.

The ground got closer and closer. Tom could make out the small figure of Elenna, with Storm and Silver, on the path where he had left her.

Looking up, Tom felt a shock of fear run through his veins. The muscular figure of Koraka broke through the clouds and come hurtling down on

them, her spear at the ready.

The Beast was back, and she
wanted her prey.

CHAPTER EIGHT

THE USELESS TOKEN?

Fredo screamed and clutched harder at Tom as Koraka fastened her talons around the edges of the shield, halting their flight. She beat her wings, screeching with fury, and thrashed Tom and Fredo from side to side.

Tom looked down. It was only a short drop to the ground, and Elenna stood beneath them, no

more than a blur in Tom's sight
as Koraka swung him to and fro.

"Can you catch Fredo?" Tom
shouted to his friend.

"I think so!" Elenna said.

"Let go," Tom told the boy.

But Fredo shook his head,
squeezing his eyes shut and gripping
Tom even tighter. "I can't," he
whimpered. "I'm too scared."

Tom cast a fearful look up at the
Beast above him. Koraka let out
a triumphant shriek as she tugged
with her talons, taking them a little
higher in the air – making Fredo's
drop more dangerous. He also knew
that he hadn't a hope of defeating
her with a small boy clinging to him.

Using what strength he could
muster, Tom threw his bodyweight
downwards, hoping to sink a little

lower. They had only seconds before the Beast flew back to her nest, taking him and Fredo with her.

Then Tom had an idea. With his free hand, he began tickling Fredo under the ribs. The boy let out a squeal and his grip on Tom loosened. Arms flailing, he plummeted towards Elenna, who caught him safely, rolling over with him on the grass.

Tom saw Elenna and Fredo scramble to their feet. Koraka yanked on his shield, lifting him higher into the air, closer to the mountainside. With a flick of her talons, she slammed Tom against the steep slope.

The impact jarred his bones and he couldn't hang onto his shield. He felt gravity seize him as he tumbled down the steep slope on his back. Ahead he saw the cliff drop away.

I'm going to die! Tom thought.

Desperately Tom drew his sword and rolled over. A moment before he would have plummeted to his death, he drove the blade into a crack in the stone. His body jerked to a stop as he hung off the hilt, legs dangling over nothingness. Panting, he looked up. He'd saved his own life, but without his shield he was vulnerable.

Koraka dived at him, her spear outstretched. Still gripping the sword,

Tom swung to one side as she stabbed. Splinters of stone stung his skin as the spear-point hit the rock.

I can't keep this up for long, he thought. *I'll get tired soon – or Koraka will find her range and skewer me.*

"Tom!" Elenna's voice came from below. "Which token should I use?"

Dodging another of Koraka's attacks, Tom looked down. Elenna had thrown her bow aside – arrows were no use with Koraka so far out of range. Instead, Tom's friend was rummaging frantically through Storm's saddlebags, pulling out the tokens that would defeat the Beasts of Seraph.

Elenna fetched out the chainmail and cast it to one side. Tom realised that would be no use: Elenna couldn't throw it to him all the way up the mountain.

Then she pulled out the knife, and glanced upwards, as if she was wondering whether she could hit the Beast from where she stood.

"No, that won't work!" Tom yelled.

While he was distracted, Koraka swooped with an ear-splitting shriek. Tom barely had time to scramble out of the way before her spear sank deep into the cliff-face near where he clung to his sword hilt.

When he looked back at Elenna his friend had taken out the bottle of poison, but she barely glanced at it before she put it back in the bag. Like the knife and the chainmail, there was no way of getting it to Tom.

Then Elenna pulled the jade whistle out of the saddlebag.

That must be it! Tom thought, daring

to hope. *The sound must have some sort of effect on Koraka.*

"Try it, Elenna!" he yelled.

Elenna put the whistle to her lips and blew. Just as when she'd first tried it, back in the armoury in Avantia, there was no sound. Tom wondered if he couldn't hear it because he was too far away.

"Blow harder!" he shouted.

Elenna gave the whistle a puzzled look, then tried it again.

Still no sound.

Tom saw the gleam of Koraka's spear point once more. With a cry of effort, he swung himself round and kicked out, knocking the weapon out of Koraka's hand. Tom lost sight of it as it fell down the mountain. With a howl of rage, Koraka swooped down after it.

Tom lay panting on the ground, thankful for a few precious moments' rest. But he knew that as soon as Koraka had recovered her spear, she would be back.

If none of the tokens work, he thought, *my Quest is over!*

CHAPTER NINE

HELP ON THE WING

Tom gritted his teeth with determination. *I can't let Malvel win! Not after I've defeated him so many times.*

Koraka reappeared, soaring into the sky just above Tom with powerful wing-beats. Her spear flashed down again, aimed straight at Tom's throat. Tom heaved himself out of the way, but Koraka lifted the spear away at the last moment, and snatched Tom in her razor-sharp claw.

She tricked me! he realised.

As Koraka began to lift off, Tom wrenched his sword blade out of the ground and aimed a desperate swing at her wing. He felt the blade strike – several of the Beast's feathers fluttered down.

Koraka shrieked in pain. For a moment her wingbeats faltered and she began to lose height – but then she soared again, heading back up the mountainside towards her nest.

There must be some way to defeat this Beast! Tom thought.

But he didn't know what he could do. Koraka's claws clutched him tighter and tighter until he couldn't breathe. His vision was speckled with swirling black spots, and he knew he

was only seconds away from
losing consciousness.

*She's going to squeeze the life right
out of my body!*

Tom suddenly realised that he
wasn't quite blacking out yet. There
were black spots in front of his eyes

and they were growing larger.

A flock of birds had appeared in the distance, flying straight for Koraka.

What's happening? Tom wondered. *We haven't seen any birds at all, and now there's a whole flock of them.*

Then he understood. The jade whistle!

If his arms weren't pinned to his sides by the Beast, Tom would have punched the air. He remembered how the whistle had made Silver roll over back in Avantia. Only animals could hear it. The whistle had sent a silent bird-call to the noble winged creatures of Seraph.

As they drew closer, Tom made out huge crows with shining black wings, falcons with hooked beaks and glittering eyes, gulls whose feathers shone silver, and all kinds of smaller birds as well: sparrows, starlings, larks and pigeons. They whirled down from the sky in a riot of feathers. Cawing and shrieking, they surrounded Koraka, pecking at her fiercely and battering at her with their wings, beaks and talons.

Koraka fought back, striking out with her spear, but the birds simply wheeled away for a moment, and then resumed their attack. Tom took in huge gulps of air as he felt the grip of the Beast's claws slacken.

He looked down as Koraka lurched in the air, her wing-strokes clumsy as the birds got in her way. The ground spiralled closer. The fitful lurching became a faster plunge, with Koraka spinning back and forth as she tried to avoid the birds.

The ground wheeled sickeningly

around Tom. He caught glimpses of walls and rooftops, and realised that the Beast's flight had dragged her back towards the market town. People were standing in the streets, pointing upwards at the battle above their heads.

Struggling against the birds, Koraka had lost all control. The ground rushed up towards Tom at a tremendous rate. He managed to wriggle his other arm free so that he could grip his sword in both hands.

I've got to break free…or I'll be crushed under her body when she hits the ground.

Raising his sword, Tom hacked at the Beast's wing again. Koraka's grip loosened and he felt himself beginning to fall faster. With all his strength, Tom kicked off against the Beast's body, diving to his right as far

as he could. His body turned upside down until he couldn't see where he was going to land. The mass air battle between Koraka and the birds of Seraph was just a blur, a writhing black cloud crashing to the ground.

"Ooof!"

Tom felt not the hard Seraph land, but wood beneath his body. It broke apart and he fell through it, splinters and jagged edges scratching at his clothes and skin.

With another gasp of pain, his body slammed down on the floor inside a wooden shack. As Tom struggled to his feet, he heard a noise like a thunderclap from outside. He felt the earth shudder beneath his feet, and knew that the flock of birds had succeeded in dragging Koraka to the ground.

If the Beast is dead, he thought, horror flooding through him, *does that mean that the good person inside her is dead, too?*

CHAPTER TEN

THE BEAST DEFEATED

Tom thrust aside the sagging planks –
all that was left of the walls of the
wrecked shack – and fought his way
to the door. As he stepped outside, he
almost tripped over something. He
looked down and saw Koraka's spear.
*She must have dropped it in the last
moments of her struggle*, he realised.

Picking up the spear, Tom looked

around. Not far away, a small cluster of townspeople were drifting towards something lying on the ground.

"Did you see that?" someone asked. "It fell right out of the sky!"

"Don't go too close," a woman said, grabbing the arm of a small girl.
"It might still be dangerous."

"Tom! Tom!"

Tom spun round as he heard his name being called. Elenna was riding up on Storm, with Fredo sitting in front of her and Silver bounding alongside. The grey wolf let out an excited howl as he ran up to Tom. Elenna had retrieved Tom's shield too. It hung in its usual place on the saddle.

"Tom, are you all right?" Elenna demanded. She jumped down from Storm and lifted Fredo to the ground.

Tom winced; he could still feel his bruises from the fall. "I will be," he replied. "And we're one step closer to rescuing Seraph from Malvel's evil magic."

Turning back to the townspeople, Tom saw that they were edging towards the body of the Beast. The birds stood around her in a wide and watchful circle.

Is Koraka dead? Tom asked himself, feeling sick with despair.

At the same moment the Beast suddenly sprang up, screeching wildly as she broke through the barrier of birds. Her wings and arms raised, she bore down on the terrified knot of townspeople, her claws ready to rip them apart. She loomed over a clutch of old women.

"No!" Tom cried, throwing the

spear on instinct. It whistled though
the air and punched through
Koraka's left wing, then stabbed
into the earth.

Koraka was pinned to the ground.
She writhed to free herself, but it was
no good – the spear held her fast.

As Tom ran up with his sword at
the ready, he saw a curious purple
liquid trickling from one of the

Beast's human arms where the
spear had grazed it.

The evil magic, Tom realised.

"Where is my son?"

Tom looked to his right to see Cris,
Fredo's father, stepping out of the
crowd and making for Koraka,
a knife in his hand. "You killed my
boy, monster!" he bellowed

"Cris, no!" Tom said, starting for

the man but knowing he wouldn't reach him in time to stop the slaughter.

"Father!"

Cris whirled around at Fredo's voice. He dropped the knife and bound over to the boy, sweeping him up into his arms. "Fredo!"

Tom breathed a sigh of relief, then turned back to the Beast. He gasped in amazement to see she had begun to change.

Her claws shrank and disappeared, becoming ordinary human feet, her legs the perfect size for her torn trousers. Her feathered tail and her wings melted away, leaving slender arms. Rich brown hair sprouted from her head and tumbled down her back, while her gaping mouth closed up to form a woman's lips. Soon all that lay before them was a woman in tattered, filthy clothes. The only thing that reminded Tom of the Beast were her striking green eyes.

The crowd of townspeople stared as the transformation took place.

"Cora?" Cris muttered. "Is that you?"

"So that's the missing shepherdess!" Elenna exclaimed, coming to stand next to Tom. "We should have guessed!"

"That purple liquid must have been Malvel's poison," Tom said. "Now it's gone, she's human again."

Cora stumbled to her feet, looking around in bewilderment.

"Where am I?" she asked. "How did I get here?"

"That's a long story," Tom replied with a grin.

An older woman came out of the

crowd and put her arms comfortingly around Cora. "Come home with me, dear," she said. "You need a good rest."

The shepherdess went with her without protest, still looking confused.

Cris pushed his way towards Tom and hugged him. "You saved my son," he told Tom. "Whatever I have is yours."

"I was glad to do it," Tom replied.

"You must both stay with me tonight," Cris went on. "And we'll share that pot of parsnip soup!"

When he had thanked Cris, Tom withdrew a couple of paces, to where Elenna stood with Storm and Silver. He hesitated for a moment, gazing at the townspeople, who were letting out joyful cries as they crowded around Cora, Cris and Fredo.

"They think it's all over," he said quietly. "But it's not."

Elenna nodded. "I know. Malvel is getting closer and closer to the Eternal Flame. If he manages to burn the Warlock's Staff there, then he'll make everyone in Seraph his slave."

Letting out a long sigh, Tom turned away from the happy townspeople and mounted Storm.

"We'll eat tonight," he said, as he helped Elenna up behind him. "We need to build up our strength. But tomorrow, we continue our journey – there are more Beasts out there, waiting for us. And we have to defeat every one of them."

As they trotted along the road to Cris's cottage, Tom knew there were harder battles to come.

Join Tom on the next stage
of the Beast Quest when he meets

SILVER
THE WILD TERROR

Win an exclusive
Beast Quest T-shirt and goody bag!

Tom has battled many fearsome Beasts and we want to know which one is your favourite! Send us a drawing or painting of your favourite Beast and tell us in 30 words why you think it's the best.

Each month we will select **three** winners to receive a Beast Quest T-shirt and goody bag!

Send your entry on a postcard to
BEAST QUEST COMPETITION
Orchard Books, 338 Euston Road, London NW1 3BH.

Australian readers should email:
childrens.books@hachette.com.au

New Zealand readers should write to:
Beast Quest Competition, 4 Whetu Place, Mairangi Bay,
Auckland NZ, or email: childrensbooks@hachette.co.nz

**Don't forget to include your name and address.
Only one entry per child.**

Good luck!

Join the Quest,
Join the Tribe

www.beastquest.co.uk

Have you checked out the Beast Quest website?
It's the place to go for games, downloads, activities,
sneak previews and lots of fun!

You can read all about your favourite Beasts, down-
load free screensavers and desktop wallpapers for
your computer, and even challenge your friends
to a Beast Tournament.

Sign up to the newsletter at www.beastquest.co.uk
to receive exclusive extra content and the oppor-
tunity to enter special members-only competitions.
We'll send you up-to-date info on all the Beast
Quest books, including the next exciting series
which features six brand-new Beasts!

Get 30% off all Beast Quest Books at www.beastquest.co.uk
Enter the code BEAST at the checkout.

Offer valid in UK and ROI, offer expires December 2013

All books priced at £4.99,
special bumper editions
priced at £5.99.

Orchard Books are available from all good bookshops, or can
be ordered from our website: www.orchardbooks.co.uk,
or telephone 01235 827702, or fax 01235 8227703.

Series 9: THE WARLOCK'S STAFF
COLLECT THEM ALL!

Malvel is up to his evil tricks again! The fate of all the lands is in Tom's hands...

URSUS
THE CLAWED ROAR

978 1 40831 316 9

MINOS
THE DEMON BULL

978 1 40831 317 6

KORAKA
THE WINGED ASSASSIN

978 1 40831 318 3

SILVER
THE WILD TERROR

978 1 40831 319 0

SPIKEFIN
THE WATER KING

978 1 40831 320 6

TORPIX
THE TWISTING SERPENT

978 1 40831 321 3

Series 10: Master of the Beasts
Out March 2012

Meet six terrifying new Beasts!

Noctila the Death Owl
Shamani the Raging Flame
Lustor the Acid Dart
Voltrex the Two-Headed Octopus
Tecton the Armour-Plated Giant
Doomskull the King of Fear

**Watch out for the next Special Bumper Edition Grashkor the Death Guard!
OUT JAN 2012!**

SPECIAL BUMPER EDITION!

978 1 40831 517 0